POWERFUL AND PONGY
CONTENTS

PLOP

PRECIOUS PLANTS

From prickly cacti to bushy ferns, there are around 375,000 species of plant. What do they have in common? Most plants are green and have an amazing superpower: they make their own food.

HOW DO PLANTS MAKE FOOD?

Plants make food from three ingredients: sunlight, water and carbon dioxide, which is a gas they absorb from the air. Sunlight is a type of energy given off by the Sun. Plants soak up sunlight using a green chemical called chlorophyll, which is why most plants look green. Using this energy, plants change carbon dioxide and water into sugar and oxygen. This superpower is called photosynthesis, which means 'making from light' in Greek.

Carbon dioxide

Energy

Oxygen

Sugar (made inside leaves)

Water

FREAKY FACT

The oldest living thing is believed to be a bristlecone pine that is over 5,000 years old. These trees grow in stony soils in parts of the USA where there is little rain.

Stupendous and Tremendous SCIENCE

POWERFUL (AND PONGY) PLANTS

ENTER A WORLD OF FANTASTIC FLORA!

Claudia Martin

WAYLAND

First published in Great Britain in 2022 by Wayland

Copyright © Hodder and Stoughton Limited, 2022

Produced for Wayland by
White-Thomson Publishing Ltd
www.wtpub.co.uk

Author and editor: Claudia Martin
Series Designer: Rocket Design (East Anglia) Ltd
Illustrator: Steve Evans

HB ISBN: 978 1 5263 1607 3
PB ISBN: 978 1 5263 1620 2

Wayland
An imprint of
Hachette Children's Group
Part of Hodder & Stoughton
Carmelite House
50 Victoria Embankment
London EC4Y 0DZ

An Hachette UK Company
www.hachette.co.uk
www.hachettechildrens.co.uk

Printed in China

Absolutely horrid pongy stench!

Illustrations by Steve Evans: front cover main, 2, 5c, 9b, 11tr, 11b, 13cl, 17cl, 17cr, 20cr, 21c, 22t, 25cl, 26b, 28b, 29t, 29c, 29b, 31br.

Picture acknowledgements: iStock: blueringmedia 4; Shutterstock: BudOlga front cover tr, back cover cl, GraphicsRF.com front cover b/g, 1, 7cr, drawkman 3t, 16c, 30tl, Gabi Wolf 3b, Nickolay Stanev 5r, Excellent Dream 6, Basjan Bernard 7tr, Africa Studio 7cl, Budai Romi 7b, Bahdanovich Alena 8, Studio Barcelona 9t, Unicus 9cr, Dobryanska Olga 10tl, Ortis 10tr, Oleg Krugliak 10c, Julia Sudnitskaya 10bl, Muellek Josef 10br, Vecton 12, Christian Vinces 13cr, Sari ONeal 13br, Flower Studio 13bc, MicroOne 14–15c, Vector Tradition 14t, Daniel Prudek 14br, Yayayoyo 15tr, Ondrej Prosicky 15cl, Drosophila Photograph 15c, Nattanan726 15cr, Danita Delimont 15b, taveesak srisomthavil 17c, Tetiana Maltseva 17br, Jason Finn 18cr, Robert Neumann 18cl, K.Pock Pics 18br, ervin herman 18bl, AlexeyZet 19tr, DSLucas 19bl, Henri Koskinen 20bl, lorenza62 20br, Kuttelvaserova Stuchelova 21bl, Kris Wiktor 21br, Aysezgicmeli 22bc, Muh Sahal Mahadi 22br, plasid 23tr, I. Rottlaender 23cl, jflin98 23cr, nnattalli 23bl, KatyGr5 24cr, 32br, Volodymyr Nikolaiev 24br, Tiger Images 24bc, Lubava 24br, Zmiter 25tr, 32t, Gavran333 25bl, Egor Rodynchenko 25bc, Subject Photo 25br, Shanvood 26cl, Jerry Horbert 27tl, Tjis 27tr, Jiang Tianmu 27cl, Ion Mes 27cr.
All additional design elements from Shutterstock or drawn by designer.

Every effort has been made to clear copyright. Should there be any inadvertent omission, please apply to the publisher for rectification.

The website addresses (URLs) included in this book were valid at the time of going to press. However, it is possible that contents or addresses may have changed since the publication of this book. No responsibility for any such changes can be accepted by either the author or the publisher.

All facts and statistics were up to date at the time of press.

WHAT'S THE POINT OF PLANTS?

By changing sunlight into food, plants create a type of energy that animals can use: sugar. Plant-eating animals eat plants to get energy to live ... and that energy is passed on to the meat-eaters that eat them! On top of that, when plants photosynthesise, they release oxygen. Without photosynthesis there would be no oxygen in the air. Humans and other animals need oxygen to survive.

You down there! Make an effort!

Hmmm ... I still can't see it doing anything!

WHICH PLANT IS BIGGEST?

The world's biggest plant is a tree, a member of a group of plants with long woody stems called trunks. The giant sequoia grows up to 95 m (311 ft) tall with a trunk up to 47 m (155 ft) wide. The smallest flowering plant, just 1 mm (0.04 in) across, is rootless duckweed, which floats on ponds.

GIANT GENERAL

The world's biggest giant sequoia is found in California, USA. It is called General Sherman.

DIDDY DUCKWEED

Rootless duckweed

★★★★
GENERAL SHERMAN

DARING to be DIFFERENT

With a little sunlight, warmth and water, plants can survive in habitats from oceans to deserts. Yet in different habitats, plants have found different ways to survive – which has given us a marvellous mix of plants!

Vein

Leaf

Leaf bud

Stem

Tiny tubes

Root

Root hair

DO ALL PLANTS HAVE THE SAME PARTS?

Most – but not all – plants have roots, stems and leaves. Although they look surprisingly different from each other, roses, trees, grasses and ferns all have these parts. These are vascular plants, which have roots to draw up water from the soil and tiny tubes to transport it around their body.

There are around 310,000 species of vascular plant.

DO ALL PLANTS FLOWER?

Most vascular plants have flowers. Flowers produce seeds, which contain the embryo of a new plant. Non-flowering plants make seeds without the help of flowers. Many, including conifers, produce seeds in cones. Others, such as ferns, reproduce by releasing spores instead of seeds. Spores are tinier and simpler than seeds.

I thought ALL plants had flowers!

Conifer cone

My seeds will fall out if you shake me!

SHAKE IT OUT!

Fern

Spores

SURELY ALL PLANTS HAVE ROOTS?

In fact, there are around 65,000 species of rootless plant, including mosses. They usually live in damp places or in water, so they can soak up water through hair-like rhizoids. If these plants live on land, their rhizoids also anchor them to the ground. These simple plants reproduce using spores.

Moss

SUPER SCIENCE

Syntrichia caninervis is a moss that survives in deserts, where it hardly ever rains. Since *Syntrichia* has no roots, it collects tiny drops of water from fog in its cup-like, hairy leaves. This method of water-collection is being borrowed by scientists to build machines that supply drinking water to people in dry regions.

GET to the ROOT of IT

Roots hold a plant in place and soak up water through their thin, hair-like tips. Whether super-long or stealthy, roots have many ways to get the job done.

WHICH PLANT HAS THE LONGEST ROOTS?

Roots also allow a plant to soak up nutrients, such as nitrogen, which are found in soil. In dry areas, many plants have long roots that grow deep underground. They are able to reach water that lies far beneath the dry surface soil. The longest roots belong to rye, which has coiled, thread-like roots up to 623 km (387 miles) long.

Rye is a grass grown for its small fruits, called cereal grains, which are used to make bread.

SUPER SCIENCE

Scientists believe plants communicate by releasing chemicals through their roots. For example, some chemicals warn surrounding plants of an insect pest.

The idea of communication between things that don't have brains is inspiring scientists who design robots to work together in factories. It shows how simple signals can help a group of robots respond to a changing situation.

Psst, pass it on ...

DO ALL ROOTS GROW IN SOIL?

Some plants have roots that grow above ground, often wrapping around another plant for support. These roots usually soak up water from the air, so they are more common in misty rainforests. A few, stealthy plants, known as parasites, have roots that actually pierce other plants, taking water and nutrients from them.

BIT CLINGY

This orchid's roots are wrapped around a tree, but it takes water from the air.

PESKY PARASITE

A mistletoe's roots suck water and nutrients from a tree.

Ha! I don't even say thank you!

I don't remember agreeing to this ...

WHY DO SOME PLANTS STRANGLE OTHERS?

Strangler fig trees grow in tall forests where small plants struggle to get enough sunlight. To solve the problem, strangler fig seeds start growing in crevices in the branches of tall trees, where they are dropped by fig-eating birds. As strangler figs get bigger, their roots grow downwards, wrapping around their host tree to reach the ground.

LEAVE IT!

Leaves are busy factories where the work of photosynthesis is done. They take in carbon dioxide from the air through tiny holes called stomata. Water and food are carried to and fro along tubes called veins.

ARE ALL LEAVES THE SAME?

Leaves have many different shapes and sizes. Scientists divide leaves into basic groups:

SIMPLE

Found on many flowering plants, these broad, flat leaves are attached directly to a twig or stem by a stalk, called a petiole.

COMPOUND

Also found on flowering plants, these leaves have several leaflets attached to their petiole.

SHEATH

These leaves wrap the stems of grasses.

SCALE

These triangular leaves, which look a bit like fish scales, are found on conifers, such as cypresses.

NEEDLE

Found on conifers such as firs, these leaves are long and thin.

WHY DO SOME TREES LOSE THEIR LEAVES IN AUTUMN?

In regions with short but cold winters, such as the UK, many trees have simple or compound leaves. These soak up lots of sunlight during summer, but are too delicate to survive the winter, so they are dropped from the tree in autumn. Trees that drop their leaves are called deciduous trees. In colder regions, most trees are conifers with tough needle-shaped leaves that can survive long winters.

I'm turning over a new leaf!

WHICH PLANT HAS THE BIGGEST LEAVES?

The biggest leaves, up to 25 m (82 ft) long, grow on the royal raffia palm of tropical regions of Africa. They are compound leaves, made up of 180 leaflets.

Size isn't everything!

 SUPER SCIENCE

Leaves grow from stems in special patterns, often on alternating sides or in spirals. These arrangements mean that no leaf is in another's shade.

Solar panels are devices that soak up sunlight to turn it into electricity. The designers of solar panel installations have copied leaf arrangements to make sure their panels catch as much light as possible.

FIERCE FLOWERS

Flowers are how flowering plants reproduce. They are where male pollen meets female ovules. From whopping flowers to whiffy flowers, they have more to offer than just pretty petals.

ARE FLOWERS MALE OR FEMALE?

Most flowers are both male and female. They have male stamens that make pollen. They also have a pistil that contains the female parts. The pistil is made up of a stigma, which is sticky to catch pollen; a style, which connects the stigma with the ovary; and the ovary, holding ovules. Some plants, such as cucumbers, have flowers that are only male or only female.

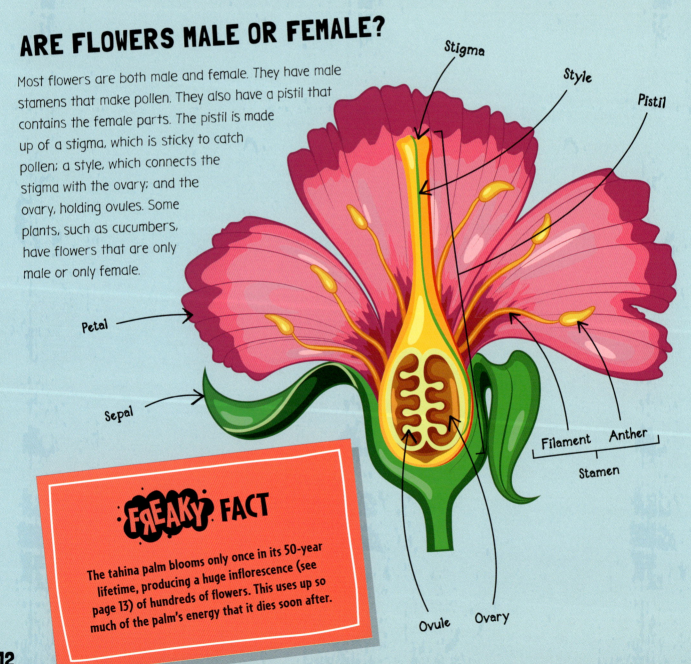

Stigma

Style

Pistil

Petal

Sepal

Filament   Anther

Stamen

Ovule   Ovary

FREAKY FACT

The tahina palm blooms only once in its 50-year lifetime, producing a huge inflorescence (see page 13) of hundreds of flowers. This uses up so much of the palm's energy that it dies soon after.

WHICH FLOWER IS THE BIGGEST?

The largest single flower belongs to the corpse lily, named for the fact the bloom smells like rotting meat. The flower reaches 105 cm (41 in) wide. Some plants produce inflorescences, which are clusters of flowers on a single stem. The largest inflorescence, up to 8 m (26 ft) tall, is made by the titanka plant.

The titanka is found in the Andes regions of Bolivia and Peru, in South America.

Blurrgh!

The corpse lily smells unattractive to humans, but it attracts insects, such as flies that like to feed on rotting meat.

Absolutely horrid pongy stench!

WHICH FLOWER HAS THE MOST PETALS?

The highest number of petals on any wild flower is 12, but garden roses have been bred by humans to have more. The flowers of sunflowers and daisies seem to have more petals, but they are actually inflorescences: their 'petals' are separate flowers around a central disk of many more flowers.

Garden rose

1ST PRIZE

Common daisy

POWERFUL POLLINATION

Pollination is when pollen is carried from the male parts to the female parts of a flower. Usually pollen is carried to a different flower in the same species. Pollination takes place in strange and surprising ways.

HOW FAR CAN POLLEN TRAVEL?

Some flowers rely on the wind or on water, such as streams, seas and rain, to carry their pollen to another flower. When carried by strong winds or oceans, pollen can travel many thousands of kilometres.

WHICH ANIMALS ARE POLLINATORS?

Many flowers use animals, called pollinators, to carry their pollen. To attract pollinators, these flowers make nectar, a sugary liquid. When a pollinator feeds on nectar, pollen is caught on their fuzz, fur or feathers, then rubs off on the next flower they visit. Flowers make sure they attract their particular pollinators by having bright petals, which may also give off an attractive smell. Up to 200,000 different animal species, most of them insects, are pollinators of the 295,000 species of flowering plant.

HELPFUL HONEYBEE

Honeybees use nectar to make honey.

WHICH FLOWERS GO IT ALONE?

A few flowers pollinate themselves, by having stamens that reach their stigma. These plants often grow in harsh places, such as the Arctic or high mountains, where there are few animals to be pollinators.

Hi, Petal.

I would like to be alone.

Yum

BENEFICIAL BAT

A long-nosed bat drinks from agave blossom.

MARVELLOUS MOTH

Moths often like pale flowers with a strong smell.

LOVELY LEMUR

In Madagascar, the black and white ruffed lemur drinks nectar from the traveller's palm plant.

HANDY HUMMINGBIRD

Hummingbirds have long beaks for sipping nectar.

FREAKY FACT

The flower of the mirror orchid looks and smells like a female scoliid wasp. Using this trick, it attracts male scoliid wasps to pollinate it.

WEIRD FRUIT

After pollination, a flower's ovules turn into seeds and its ovary becomes a fruit. The fruit may be fleshy, as in a plum, or hard, as in a nut. Some fruits, such as raspberries, are made of several ovaries joined together.

ARE ALL FRUITS EDIBLE?

Many fruits are tiny, dry or poisonous to humans. Yet lots of fruits – from apples to bananas – are healthy to eat and taste sweetly delicious. Some edible fruits are savoury-tasting: cucumbers, pumpkins and wheat grains are also fruits. For a plant, producing edible fruits is a way to spread its seeds far and wide, so that baby plants do not grow in their parent's shadow. After munching a fruit, an animal spits or poos out the seeds, which can then start to grow.

In one end ...

PLOP

... and out the other ... YIPPEE!

FREAKY FACT

Rather than waiting to be eaten, the fruit of the sandbox tree explodes when it is ripe. The seeds are thrown up to 45 m (148 ft) from the tree.

BOOM!

WHICH FRUIT SMELLS LIKE POO ... OR CUSTARD?

In Southeast Asia, the durian fruit is known for its strong smell, which attracts animals including tigers and orangutans from nearly a kilometre away. While some people describe the smell as like custard or caramel, others describe it as poo, vomit or rotten onions. These different responses are due to the fruit's complex mix of chemicals.

The durian's thorny coating discourages small animals, but large animals can break open the fruit, then carry its seeds far away.

Mmm, custard.

Eww, poo.

WHICH FRUIT HAS THE MOST SEEDS?

The pomegranate fruit has the most seeds, up to 1,400. It is produced from a single ovary that contains many ovules. At the other end of the scale, a few plants can produce fruits without being pollinated, making seedless fruits that cannot grow into new plants. Seedless fruits are easy to eat, so humans sometimes grow more of these plants by cutting sprigs and planting them. That is why we have seedless satsumas!

Count my seeds! Go on!

STRANGE SEEDS

Inside a tough coating, a seed holds an unformed baby plant and a little food. A seed will not start to sprout until it is in a suitable spot. Plants have weird ways of helping their seeds find that spot.

WHAT STRANGE METHODS DO PLANTS USE TO SPREAD SPEEDS?

Edible fruits are not the only method of spreading seeds over a wide area:

TUMBLING

Tumbleweed plants separate from their roots so they can be blown along, spreading seeds as they go.

BLOWING

After pollination, dandelion flowers turn into seed heads with many tiny fruits, each attached to a superlight umbrella to lift it on the wind.

Plants that live by rivers or oceans often produce floating fruits or seeds.

FLOATING

ANTS!

Some plants make seeds with fleshy lumps attached to them. Ants collect the seeds, eat the lumps, then leave the seeds to grow.

WHY ARE FORGETFUL SQUIRRELS USEFUL?

Squirrels like to eat nuts, which are hard fruits. When acorns and hazelnuts ripen in autumn, squirrels bury some to eat during winter. The problem for squirrels is that they forget where they buried all their nuts! But the lost acorns and hazelnuts may grow into oak and hazel trees.

Now where did I leave it ...?

WHICH SEED TOOK LONGEST TO START GROWING?

Seeds do not start to grow, or germinate, until the levels of warmth and water are just right. Water or heat cracks the seed's coating, after a few days, weeks or even years. The seeds that took the longest to germinate belonged to date palms. They were left in desert caves in what is now Israel, around 2,000 years ago. After being found by scientists, the seeds were soaked and planted, then grew into trees.

SUPER SCIENCE

A bur is a seed or dry fruit that is covered in hooks. The hooks catch on animal fur, so the seed can hitch a lift away from its parent plant. In 1941, Swiss inventor George de Mestral was walking in the woods when he noticed how burs clung to his clothes and his dog's fur. They inspired him to invent Velcro®, a system for fastening clothes and shoes using two strips, one with tiny hooks and the other with loops.

I'm worth waiting for.

A date palm grows clusters of sweet fruit.

KILLER PLANTS

Some plants are not content with quietly turning sunlight into food. They need something a little bit more ... wriggly ... to keep them going. These plants use dirty tricks to meet their need for meat!

WHY DO THEY KILL?

Meat-eating plants grow in soil that is thin or boggy, so it does not contain enough nutrients to keep them healthy. They get extra nutrients from the bodies of unlucky little animals!

YIKES!

WHAT TRICKS AND TRAPS DO THEY USE?

First of all, a meat-eating plant needs to attract insects and other little creatures. It manages this with its sweet nectar, yummy smell or bright colour. Then the plant may use one of these clever – and very cruel – traps:

THE STICKY END
Prey is caught on sticky leaves.

DEATH SLIDE
Prey falls into a slippery bowl-like trap made from a rolled-up leaf.

Common sundew

CAN'T ... M-M-MOVE!

WHOA!

Northern pitcher plant

WHAT IS THE BIGGEST ANIMAL A PLANT CAN EAT?

The bigger the plant, the bigger the prey! The giant pitcher plant has a slippery bowl-shaped trap up to 40 cm (16 in) high and 20 cm (8 in) wide. Ants and other insects are its usual food, but birds, frogs, lizards and rats can all drown in the rainwater and digestive liquids that fill its deadly trap.

If hiking through the rainforest of Borneo, in Southeast Asia, watch out for the giant pitcher plant.

SUPER SCIENCE

Scientists were so impressed by the slipperiness of pitcher plants that they decided to copy them. Teams are working on new super-slippery coatings, called SLIPS (short for 'slippery liquid-infused porous surfaces'), for boats, machines and medical instruments. The coatings will stop sea creatures, dirt, ice or oil from getting stuck onto them.

THE CRUSHER
Prey makes the mistake of tickling the hairs on hinged leaves, which snap closed.

NO WAY OUT
Prey crawls inside a coiled leaf, then cannot find the exit.

THAT DIDN'T GO WELL!

Exhausted by searching for the way out, the insect will eventually tumble into this cobra lily's 'stomach'. It will be broken down by special digestive liquids, then soaked up ...

Venus flytrap

I'M IN HERE!

DON'T EAT ME!

I only want a cuddle!

Many plants put up with being nibbled by plant-eaters, but others have developed defences to stop themselves being lunch. These defences range from tough bark on tree trunks to stings, prickles and poisons.

WHICH PLANT HAS THE MOST POWERFUL STING?

The stinging brush is covered by stinging hairs. If they are touched, the hollow, sharp-tipped hairs break off and enter the skin. They inject a chemical that can cause pain for days. There are accounts of the pain from the sting coming back months or even years later.

The stinging brush grows in Australian rainforests. Don't be tempted to touch it!

WHICH CACTUS IS NO TEDDY BEAR?

The teddy bear cactus has long, sharp spines. If they get stuck in the skin of an animal, they are extremely difficult and painful to remove, because they have tiny hooks. From a distance, the spines make the cactus look furry, which earned the plant its name.

You're giving me a bad name.

Teddy bear cactus

WHICH PLANT IS THE DEADLIEST?

Many plants have poisonous fruits, seeds or other parts.
The competition for the deadliest plant is fierce:

ROSARY PEA — These seeds are sometimes used as beads, but are deadly if eaten.

DEADLY NIGHTSHADE — Both leaves and berries are poisonous.

WATER HEMLOCK — All parts of this plant are poisonous, but the roots are deadliest.

TOBACCO — The dried leaves are used in cigarettes, which can cause cancer and diseases of the heart and lungs.

 FACT

The plant with the longest thorns, over 20 cm (8 in) long, is the North American honey locust. Thorns are branches or stems that, over millions of years, have evolved to be sharp.

FUNKY FEEDERS

We should all eat plenty of plant parts in the form of cereal grains, fruits and vegetables. These give us energy, protein for growing, vitamins and minerals for health, and fibre to help keep our digestive systems healthy.

WHICH PLANT DO HUMANS EAT MOST?

The small, dry fruit of the rice plant is the food most eaten by humans. Across much of the world, rice is a staple food, which is a food eaten often and in large quantities. Close behind rice are two other cereal grains: maize and wheat.

I'm feeding the world!

WHICH PART OF A PLANT IS A VEGETABLE?

The foods we call vegetables come from many different plant parts:

ROOTS

Carrots are swollen roots, where the plant stores food to survive winter.

STEMS

Potatoes are swollen underground stems, called tubers, which last through winter when the above-ground plant dies. They can grow into a new plant in spring.

BULBS

Onions are swollen underground stems and leaves, called bulbs.

HOW MANY SEEDS IN A BAR OF CHOCOLATE?

Around 50 seeds, called cocoa beans, go into making one snack-sized bar of chocolate, along with milk, sugar and oil. Around 30 to 50 seeds form in each pod on a cocoa tree. The tree grows naturally only in hot parts of the Americas, but is today also grown in Africa and Asia.

One giant leap for spud-kind.

I love seeds ...

SUPER SCIENCE

In 1995, astronauts first experimented with growing potatoes in space, aboard the Space Shuttle Columbia. Scientists are now working out how plants could be grown on Mars, where the air contains carbon dioxide but very little oxygen. Since plants make oxygen, plants might be a way to create an oxygen supply for future inhabitants of the distant planet.

LEAVES
Lettuces are floppy, crispy or curly leaves.

FRUITS
Tomatoes are fruits, even though they taste savoury.

SEEDS
Peas are seeds that grow in a fruit called a pod.

ODDLY USEFUL

Trees give wood for homes, furniture and paper. Roses and lavender scent soaps and perfume, while acacia makes glue. You are surrounded by plants, from your clothes to your medicine cabinet.

> I have hidden powers ...

WHICH MEDICINES ARE MADE FROM PLANTS?

The earliest medicines were made when people noticed that some plants helped treat fevers or wounds. Many modern medicines are still made with chemicals that come from plants, including the opium poppy, which can ease pain, and the Madagascar periwinkle, which helps treat cancer.

Like most medicinal plants, the opium poppy is both useful and extremely dangerous.

CAN PLANTS POWER CARS?

Most cars are powered by burning a fuel called oil in their engine. Since burning oil also pollutes the air, people are looking for fuels that are cleaner. One solution may be sugar cane, which can be used to make a liquid fuel that often powers cars in Brazil.

> Aren't you hungry?

WHICH PLANTS DO WE WEAR?

Plant fibres, or threads, can be woven, knitted or plaited into fabric:

The fluffy seed heads of the cotton plant are spun into cotton.

Linen is made of stem fibres from the flax plant.

COTTON

FLAX

BAMBOO

PANAMA HAT PLANT

The leaves of the Panama hat plant are used to weave ... hats.

Bamboo is a stiff-stemmed grass used to make cloth.

FREAKY FACT

Bamboo is the fastest-growing plant, reaching up to 91 cm (35 in) per day. In addition to clothing, bamboo stems are used for furniture, toothbrushes and utensils.

Bamboo →

ASTONISHING ACTIVITY:
COLOURFUL LEAVES

Try this experiment using chromatography (which means 'colour writing' in Greek). It is a method of separating mixtures. You will find out if leaves contain only green chlorophyll or a colourful mixture.

YOU WILL NEED:

10 green leaves

A glass

Surgical spirit (and an adult's help to use it)

A clothes peg

A wooden spoon

A bowl of hot tap water (and an adult's help)

A long strip of kitchen towel or coffee filter paper

1 Rip the leaves into small pieces, then place them in your glass.

2 Ask an adult to help you add enough surgical spirit to just cover the leaves. The surgical spirit will start to break down the leaves.

3 Crush the leaves into the surgical spirit using the blunt end of a wooden spoon, for about 5 minutes.

4 Without getting water inside the glass, place the glass in a bowl of hot tap water to speed things along. Put the bowl and glass in a dark place, such as a cupboard, for 30 minutes or until the surgical spirit has turned dark green.

5 Gently stir your green mixture, then place the strip of kitchen towel in the glass, with just the tip of one end in the mix. Secure it with a clothes peg if needed.

6 Watch for around 30 minutes as the paper soaks up the liquid. What is happening to the colour of the strip? When one of the colours reaches the top of the strip, remove the strip and let it dry.

COLOURFUL CONCLUSION

The chemicals in the leaves, called pigments, dissolve in the surgical spirit, so specks of pigments are floating in the liquid. As the paper soaks up the liquid, the pigments are carried with it. Some travel further up the paper because their specks are smaller and lighter. Once the pigments are separated, you can see green, yellow and orange. This experiment tells us about what happens to the leaves of deciduous trees in autumn. As the leaves stop photosynthesising, their chlorophyll breaks down, revealing the colours that are usually hidden by the overpowering green.

GLOSSARY

absorb to soak up

alternating appearing in turn

bred grown to have particular characteristics, by choosing which plants should reproduce with each other

carbon dioxide an invisible gas found in the air

cereal grain an edible, dry fruit produced by grasses such as rice, wheat, oats and maize

chlorophyll a green pigment found in plants that absorbs sunlight for photosynthesis

deciduous shedding leaves every year

dissolve to mix with a liquid

edible eatable

embryo a developing baby plant

evolve to change slowly over millions of years

fibre parts of plants that the human body cannot digest, or break down

flower the part of a seed-making plant that contains the reproductive parts

fruit the part of a plant that contains seeds and may be edible or inedible

fuel a material that can be burned to produce heat

habitat the natural home of a plant or animal

leaf a green part of a plant, where photosynthesis usually takes place, that is joined at one end to a stem or stalk

leaflet a small leaf-like structure, forming part of a compound leaf

nutrient a substance needed for growth and life

ovary a female reproductive part that will develop into a fruit

ovule the part of an ovary that will develop into a seed

oxygen an invisible gas that is made by plants

parasite a living thing that lives on or in another living thing and takes food from it

pest an insect or other animal that attacks crops

petal a special, usually colourful, leaf that surrounds the reproductive parts of a flower

photosynthesis the process by which plants produce food from sunlight, carbon dioxide and water

pigment a coloured material

pollen a powder, made by the male parts of a flower, that causes the female parts of the same species to make seeds

reproduce to make new young plants

root the part of a plant that anchors it in position and takes in water and nutrients

savoury tasting salty or spicy but not sweet

seed a small object made by a plant that can grow into a new plant

seed head the seed-containing part of some plants that develops after flowering or fruiting

species a group of living things that look similar to each other and can reproduce together

spine a sharp-pointed growth

sprig a small stem taken from a plant

stamen a male, pollen-making part of a flower

stem the main body of a plant

stigma a female part of a flower, where pollen is received

vascular with special structures for carrying water and food through the plant

vegetable any edible plant part with a savoury taste

vein a structure that carries water and food through a leaf

FURTHER READING

BOOKS

Plants (Outdoor Science)
Sonya Newland (Wayland, 2018)

Plants (Science in Infographics)
Jon Richards and Ed Simkins (Wayland, 2017)

Plants (Science Skills Sorted)
Angela Royston (Franklin Watts, 2019)

Studying Plants (Citizen Scientist)
Izzi Howell (Wayland, 2020)

The Kew Gardens Children's Cookbook: Plant, Cook, Eat
Caroline Craig (Wayland, 2016)

WEBSITES

Find out more about plants on these websites:

www.bbc.co.uk/bitesize/topics/zy66fg8

www.gardenersworld.com/how-to/grow-plants/10-gardening-projects-for-kids/

www.nhm.ac.uk/discover/plants.html

www.worldwildlife.org/places/amazon

INDEX

STUPENDOUS AND TREMENDOUS SCIENCE

TITLES IN THE SERIES

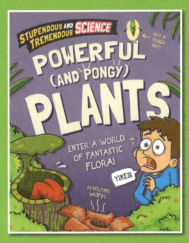

Precious Plants
Daring to Be Different
Get to the Root of It
Leave It!
Fierce Flowers
Powerful Pollination
Weird Fruit
Strange Seeds
Killer Plants
Don't Eat Me!
Funky Feeders
Oddly Useful
Astonishing Activity:
Colourful Leaves

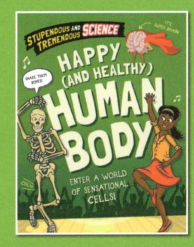

Organised Organs
Super Cells
Got It Covered
Moving Along
Lovely Lungs
Beat It!
Secret Agents
Getting Brainy
Startling Senses
Delicious Digestion
Wonderful Wee
Brilliant Babies
Astonishing Activity:
Getting a Lungful

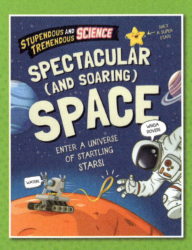

Your Universe
Extraordinary Earth
Marvellous Moon
Rocky Planets
Watch Out!
Gassy and Giant
Icy and ... Giant
Super Sun
Sparkling Stars
Gorgeous Galaxies
Up and Away!
Roaming Robots
Astonishing Activity:
Make a Bottle Rocket

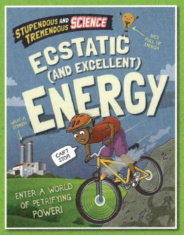

Eternal Energy
What a Star!
Feeling Hot!
Lovely Light
Shaky Shaky Sound
Crucial Chemical Energy
Moving Along ...
Lots of Potential
Exciting Electricity
Freaky Fossil Fuels
Going Nuclear
Really Renewable
Astonishing Activity:
Static Electricity Race